BATS SET II

GHOST-FACED BATS

Jill C. Wheeler
ABDO Publishing Company

visit us at
www.abdopub.com

Published by ABDO Publishing Company, 4940 Viking Drive, Edina, Minnesota 55435.
Copyright © 2006 by Abdo Consulting Group, Inc. International copyrights reserved in all
countries. No part of this book may be reproduced in any form without written permission from
the publisher. The Checkerboard Library™ is a trademark and logo of ABDO Publishing
Company.

Printed in the United States.

Cover Photo: © Merlin D. Tuttle, Bat Conservation International
Interior Photos: Animals Animals p. 13; Corbis p. 17; © Merlin D. Tuttle, Bat Conservation
    International pp. 5, 9, 11, 19, 21

Series Coordinator: Tamara L. Britton
Editors: Tamara L. Britton, Stephanie Hedlund
Art Direction, Maps, and Diagrams: Neil Klinepier

Library of Congress Cataloging-in-Publication Data

Wheeler, Jill C., 1964-
    Ghost-faced bats / Jill C. Wheeler.
        p. cm. -- (Bats. Set II)
    Includes bibliographical references (p.) and index.
    ISBN 1-59679-322-8
    1. Mormoops--Juvenile literature. I. Title.

QL737.C543W49 2005
599.4--dc22
                                                    2005043271

CONTENTS

GHOST-FACED BATS

Ghost-faced bats are one of about 900 **species** of bats. There are eight species in their **family**. Ghost-faced bats live in parts of North America, Central America, and South America.

Like all bats, ghost-faced bats are **mammals**. An amazing one-quarter of all mammals are bats. Humans are mammals, too. And, mother bats produce milk to feed their young, just like human mothers do. However, bats can fly! They are the only mammals that truly fly.

Many people think bats are scary or harmful. This is not true. Bats eat many insect pests. Some bats help **pollinate** plants or plant new trees. Bats rarely harm humans or pets. Instead, they are an important part of Earth's **ecosystem**.

Ghost-faced bats have a special chin. It has many folds of skin on it. Because of this, some people call them leaf-chinned bats or old man bats.

WHERE THEY'RE FOUND

Bats can be found all over the world. They live everywhere except for some islands and the North and South poles. Ghost-faced bats live in North, Central, and South America.

In North America, ghost-faced bats live in southern Arizona, Texas, and Mexico. In Central America, they live in Honduras and El Salvador. In South America, researchers have found ghost-faced bats in Peru, Venezuela, and Brazil. Finally, some make their homes on islands near South America's coast.

Ghost-faced bats like many different landscapes. Some live in tropical rain forests. Some live in deserts.

Others live in the area between tropical forest and pine and oak forest. Wherever ghost-faced bats are, they like it to be warm. They also want caves to live in and lots of insects to eat!

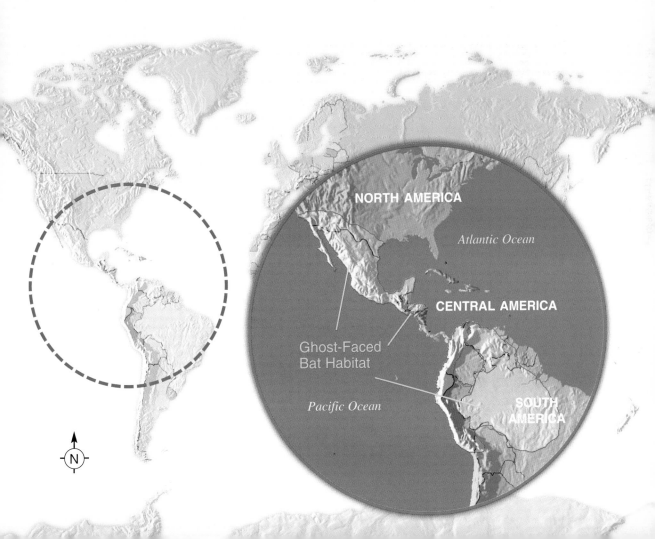

WHERE THEY LIVE

Like all bats, ghost-faced bats are **nocturnal**. They like to live in caves, but they will also **roost** in other places. They have been found living in tunnels and old mine shafts, too.

Once, four ghost-faced bats made their home in a junior high school in Texas. Students found them hanging from the ceiling. The bats had moved in during the night when the windows were open!

Ghost-faced bats do not like to be alone. They live in colonies with many other bats. Researchers found one colony of about half a million ghost-faced bats!

Even in such large colonies, ghost-faced bats do not like to roost close together. They prefer more space. Each bat hangs about six inches (15 cm) from its neighbor. Sometimes ghost-faced bats share a cave with other **species** of bats. Yet each bat group stays in a separate part of the cave.

This ghost-faced bat is roosting on a rock. Like all bats, ghost-faced bats are part of the order Chiroptera. This is a Greek word that means "hand wing." Bats have hands that are also wings!

SIZES

Bats come in many different sizes. The smallest bat is the size of a big bumblebee. So, it is called the bumblebee bat. The world's largest bats are the bat **family** called flying foxes. Some flying foxes are more than 17 inches (43 cm) long. They can have a **wingspan** of more than 5 feet (1.5 m).

Ghost-faced bats are medium-sized bats. Their bodies are 2 and a half to 3 inches (6 to 8 cm) long. They weigh around one-half of an ounce (14 g). They have a wingspan of 14 to 15 inches (36 to 38 cm).

The ghost-faced bat's ears are round and joined across its forehead. They form a pocketlike area around its eyes.

SHAPES

Ghost-faced bats are easy to spot. They have a strange, wrinkly looking face. Their fur ranges in color from dark brown to reddish brown. They have small eyes. Their large, rounded ears join across their forehead. Leaflike folds stick out from their chin.

Like humans, ghost-faced bats have arms and hands. Each hand has four fingers and a thumb with a claw. **Elastic** wing **membranes** are stretched between the bat's fingers, body, hind legs, and tail.

When the bats come home to **roost**, they hang on the ceiling. When a bat is roosting, the weight of its body pulls down on its legs. This locks its toes into position on the uneven surface. Its knees bend backward, so it can easily drop down and fly away.

Bat Anatomy

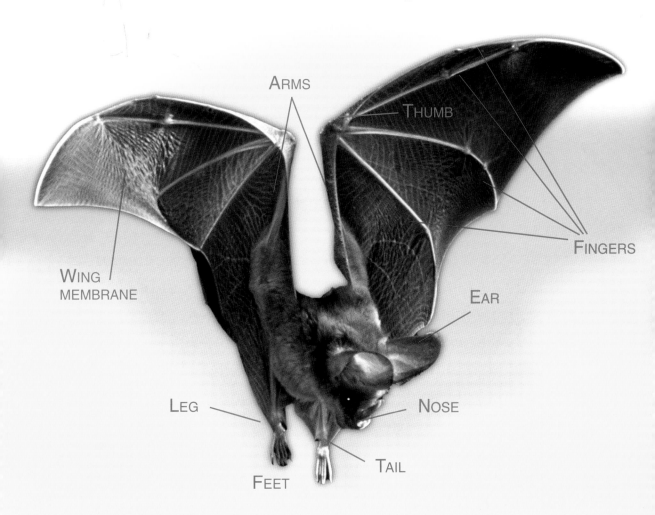

ARMS

THUMB

FINGERS

WING MEMBRANE

EAR

LEG

NOSE

FEET

TAIL

SENSES

Have you heard the phrase "blind as a bat"? This rumor probably started because bats only come out at night. Yet bats can see. They can also hear, smell, taste, and feel. About one-half of all bats have another sense called echolocation. This is how bats "see" in the dark.

To use echolocation, bats make high-pitched sounds. Some bats make these sounds from the throat, and some from the nose. These sound waves go out and bounce off an object such as a tree, building, or insect.

The echo of the sound returns to the bat. It catches the echo in its large ears. The bat uses the echo to locate an object. The echo also tells the bat how big the object is.

Humans can't hear the sounds bats make. But the bats can hear them well! Bats use echolocation to fly safely and to find food. They also use echolocation to avoid danger.

Sound wave sent out by bat

Echo wave received by bat

DEFENSE

Hawks and snakes think bats are good snacks! These **predators** often lurk outside the bats' **roosting** place. They grab the bats as they leave at dusk and return at dawn. Bats use echolocation to avoid these predators.

But, some dangers cannot be avoided by echolocation. Humans are a threat to ghost-faced bats, too. Humans can **disturb** bats in their roosts in caves and mines. Humans sometimes use **pesticides** to kill insects. Bats can get sick and die when they accidentally eat these pesticides.

Finally, humans can hurt the ghost-faced bat's **habitat**. Cutting down forests can reduce the number of insects the bats can eat. Turning forests and desert land into farmland can do the same thing.

This rain forest is being cut down. If deforestation in the rain forests continues at today's rate, in 100 years Earth will have no more rain forests. Many of the world's plant and animal species will become extinct.

FOOD

Ghost-faced bats must work to avoid **predators**. But they are predators themselves. They eat large moths and other insects.

They leave their **roosts** in large groups shortly after dark. They soar high into the sky on their way to canyons and **arroyos**. These are their favorite places to hunt.

At the hunting site, ghost-faced bats swoop down and begin picking insects out of the air. Researchers think ghost-faced bats look funny for a reason. They believe their wrinkly face and mouth hairs help funnel insects into their mouth when feeding.

Ghost-faced bats are strong, fast flyers. They catch their **prey** by flying low over water or ground. They hunt for about seven hours. Then, they return to their roosts. Humans living near hunting areas enjoy fewer insect pests thanks to ghost-faced bats!

The ghost-faced bat's long, narrow wings help it fly fast.
But, its wing membranes sometimes get torn or cut.
Luckily, the membranes heal quickly.

BABIES

To continue to contribute to the **ecosystem**, ghost-faced bats must have a safe place to reproduce. In the cave, mother bats have the warmest place. Male bats and female bats without babies live in different parts of the cave. Or, they may live in separate caves.

Female ghost-faced bats have babies in late May or early June. They have just one baby each year. Since bats are **mammals**, their babies are born alive.

Baby bats are called pups. They are quite large at birth. Some pups are one-quarter of the size of their mother! Their thumbs and feet are almost adult sized. This helps them cling to their mothers and to their **roost**.

Ghost-faced bat pups can live on their own after a few weeks. Then, they take their place as part of the ecosystem, and the process begins again.

A mother bat feeds her pup with milk. A mother bat usually
leaves her pup while she goes out to hunt. When she returns,
she finds her pup by its special smell and squeak sound.

GLOSSARY

arroyo (uh-ROY-oh) - a ditch carved by water.

disturb - to interrupt or break in upon.

ecosystem (EE-koh-sihs-tuhm) - a community of organisms and their environment.

elastic - able to return to normal shape after being stretched or bent.

family - a group that scientists use to classify similar plants or animals. It ranks above a genus and below an order.

habitat - a place where a living thing is naturally found.

mammal - an animal with a backbone that nurses its young with milk.

membrane - a thin, easily bent layer of animal tissue.

nocturnal (nahk-TUHR-nuhl) - active at night.

pesticides (PEHS-tuh-side) - chemicals used to kill insects.

pollinate - when birds and insects transfer pollen from one flower or plant to another.

predator - an animal that kills and eats other animals.

prey - animals that are eaten by other animals; also the act of seizing prey.

roost - a place, such as a cave or a tree, where bats rest during the day; also, to perch.

species (SPEE-sheez) - a kind or type.

wingspan - the distance from one wing tip to the other when the wings are spread.

WEB SITES

To learn more about ghost-faced bats, visit ABDO Publishing Company on the World Wide Web at **www.abdopub.com**. Web sites about bats are featured on our Book Links page. These links are routinely monitored and updated to provide the most current information available.

INDEX